In the Garden

GRL: B

Word count: 62

Text type: fiction

Genre: realistic fiction

High-frequency words: *a, I, in, the*

capstone
classroom

Start Reading (Capstone Classroom) is published by Capstone Press,
1710 Roe Crest Drive, North Mankato, Minnesota 56003.
www.capstoneclassroom.com

Originally published by Wayland, a division of Hachette Children's Books,
a Hachette UK company.
www.hachette.co.uk

[10 9 8 7 6 5 4 3 2 1]
Printed and bound in China.

In the Garden
ISBN 978-1-4765-3192-2

In the Garden

Written by Annemarie Young
Illustrated by Louise Redshaw

capstone
classroom

I found a butterfly
in the garden.

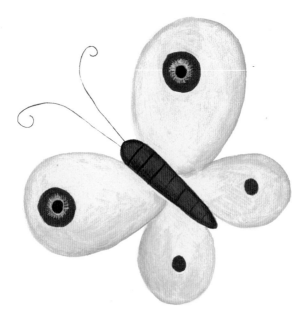

I found a ladybug
in the garden.

I found a grasshopper
in the garden.

I found a spider
in the garden.

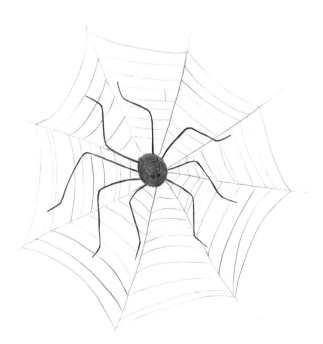

I found a beetle
in the garden.

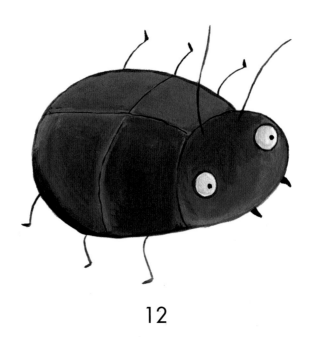

I found a dragonfly
in the garden.

I found a bee
in the garden.

I found a snail
in the garden.

I found a bug
on Dad.

In the Garden

START READING

Before reading, examine the illustrations with children, and have children locate the book title and author's name.

Preview the book

Say:
The girl and the boy show their mom and dad what they found in the garden. Then they find something on Dad!

> **Let's read the title: *In the Garden*.**
> **Look at the first page of the story. The girl is pointing.**
> **She says, "I found a butterfly in the garden."**
> **Turn the page. What does the boy say? Yes, he says, "I found a ladybug in the garden."**

Continue to page through the book, discussing the illustrations and what they tell readers about the events and the setting.

CCSS Use illustrations and details in a story to describe its characters, setting, and events. **(RL.3)**

Focus on fluency

Lead students in a choral reading, focusing on the repeated phrase: *I found a _____ in the garden*. Model how to track print as you read aloud all or part of the text with accuracy and expression. Have children follow your lead, prompting them as necessary to track print, to self-correct, and to use their knowledge of the relationships between letters and sounds to pronounce words and check meaning:

- **You said, "I saw a ladybug." The word *saw* makes sense, but take a close look at the word. The word starts with *f*. What word starts with /f/ and makes sense in the sentence? That's right—*found*!**
- **You did a great job of changing a word that didn't sound right the first time you read. That's what strategic readers do.**

CCSS Read with sufficient accuracy and fluency to support comprehension. **(RF.2)**

Focus on high-frequency words: *a, I, in, the*

Select a high-frequency word, and ask children to find it throughout the book.
- Discuss the shapes of the letters and the letter sounds.
- To memorize the word, children can write it in the air and then write it repeatedly on a whiteboard or on paper, leaving a space between each attempt to establish word boundaries.

Have children draw a picture based on the story. They can use the high-frequency words to write or talk about their pictures.

CCSS Read common high-frequency words by sight. **(RF.3)**

Connect to the Common Core

In the Garden

Prompt children's thinking about *In the Garden* with questions such as the following:

Key Ideas and Details (RL.1, RL.3)
- What animals do the children find in the garden? (butterfly, ladybug, grasshopper, spider, beetle, dragonfly, bee, snail)
- What do the children find on Dad? (a bug)

Craft and Structure (RL.6)
- Look at pages 18 and 19. Who is speaking at this point in the story? How can you tell? (The girl is speaking. She uses the word *I*, and she is showing her brother the snail.)
- Look at pages 10 and 11. Who is speaking at this point in the story? How can you tell? (The boy is speaking. He uses the word *I*, and he is showing his dad the spider.)

Integration of Knowledge and Ideas (RL.7)
- Look at the illustration on page 11. How does the boy feel about finding the spider? How can you tell? (He looks scared. He has a frown on his face, and he is standing away from the spider, pointing at it.)

Vocabulary Acquisition and Use (L.5)
- The children see a lot of insects. What other words would fit in the category of insects? Make a list. (Students might mention ants, fleas, mosquitos, stick bugs, and so on.)

Writing (W.7, W.8)
The children find many creatures in the garden. Have children list creatures they might find around their school, in their town, at a local park, or at the zoo. For each creature, have them suggest a word that describes it. Compile their list into a poem. Children can create illustrations to go with the poem.

24